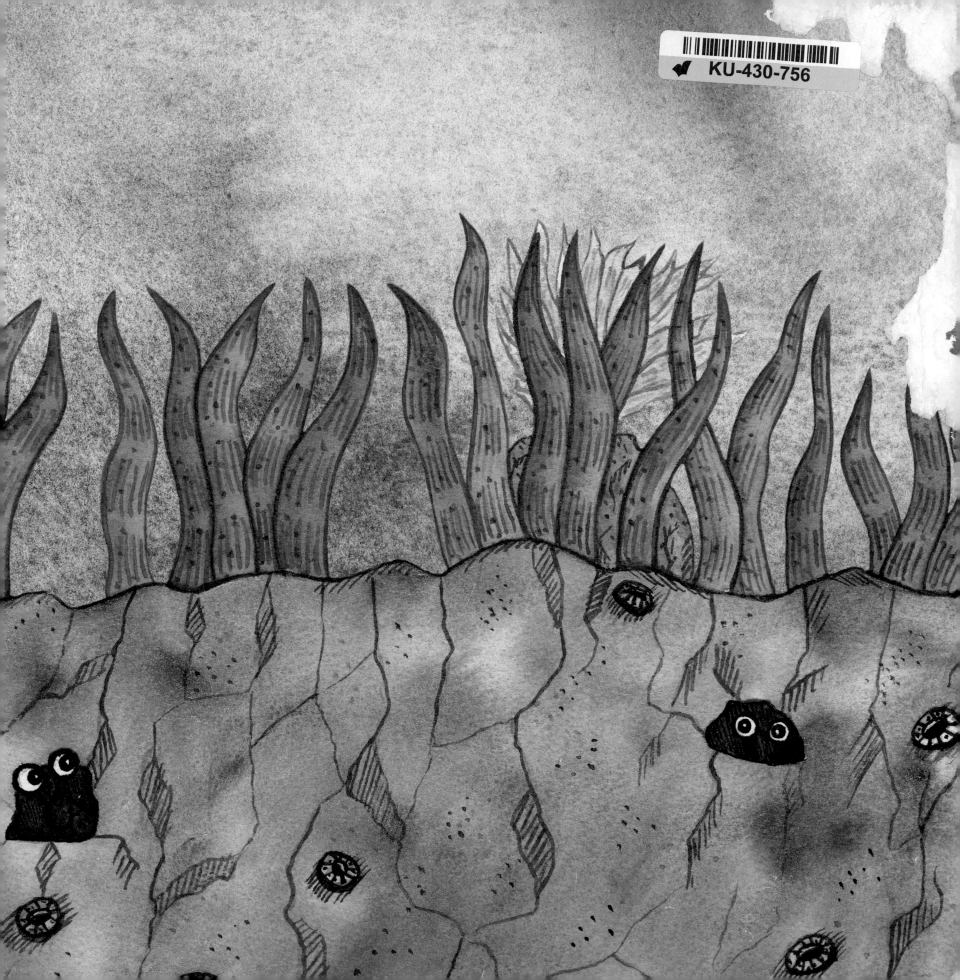

For my family - Christina, Barnaby and Matilda.

First published in Great Britain 2017 by Muddy Publishing Ltd. • www.muddypublishing.co.uk
Text and illustrations copyright © Matt Buckingham 2017 • www.mattbuckingham.co.uk
Matt Buckingham has asserted his right to be identified as the author and illustrator of this work under
the Copyright, Designs and Patents Act, 1988 • A CIP catalogue record for this book is available
from the British Library • All rights reserved

ISBN 978-1-5272-1014-1
2 4 6 8 10 9 7 5 3 1
Printed in the UK

Matt Buckingham

Bright Stanley

and the Mermaid Tale

MUDDY PUBLISHING

Far below the waves at the bottom of the sea
lived a sparkly little fish called Stanley.
   Today he had overslept and was late to meet
his friends. Again! He'd have to make up a
good excuse this time.

"Look everyone," he shouted, "over there!
I can see some **mermaid's hair!**"

The four little friends dashed to
get a closer look . . .

. . . but all they found were yellow weeds.

"Oh Stanley," sighed Percy. "For such a little fish, you've one BIG imagination. Everyone knows there are NO such things as mermaids."

The four little friends swam on and came across
a dark cave. Something was moving inside.
"Look," shouted Stanley with a wail,
"I told you so, it's a **mermaid's tail!**"

The friends crept slowly into the cave.
But it wasn't a mermaid they found inside.

"Hello Derek," giggled Pufferfish.
"So you're the mermaid Stanley had spotted!"
"Oh, Stanley!" chuckled Turtle. "See,
there are **NO** such things as mermaids!"

Stanley felt glum.

  "I really shouldn't have told that

mermaid tale," he thought.

"After all," he sighed,
"mermaids AREN'T real."

"I'm sorry for making up a tale," said Stanley
to his friends. "You're right, there are
no such things as mermaids."
"It's ok," smiled Percy. "At least you told
the truth in the end."